IZZY the WHIZ
and PASSOVER McCLEAN

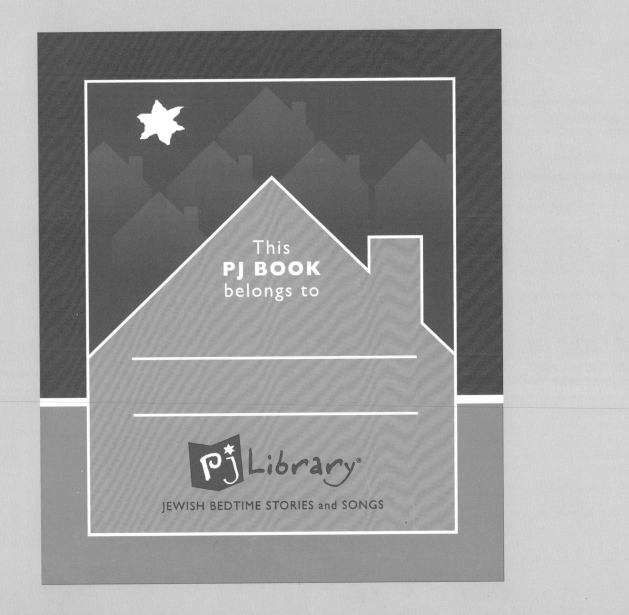

This
PJ BOOK
belongs to

pj Library®

JEWISH BEDTIME STORIES and SONGS

For Moshe, Yisrael Aryeh, Yocheved, Yitzchak, Chana and Rachel
Shira, my own little band of McCleans. – Y.M.

To Haylee and Luke – C.H.

Text copyright ©2012 by Yael Mermelstein
Illustrations copyright ©2012 by Carrie Hartman

KAR-BEN Publishing
A division of Lerner Publishing Group, Inc.
241 First Avenue North
Minneapolis, MN 55401 U.S.A.
800-4KARBEN

Website address: www.karben.com

Library of Congress Cataloging–in–Publication Data

Mermelstein, Yael.
     Izzy the Whiz and Passover McClean / by Yael Mermelstein ; illustrated
by Carrie Hartman.
          p.   cm.
     Summary: Amateur inventor Izzy creates a machine that miraculously
cleans the entire house of hametz just in time for Passover. Includes
author's note about Passover and hametz.
     ISBN 978-0-7613-5653-0 (lib. bdg. : alk. paper)
     [1. Stories in rhyme. 2. Inventions—Fiction. 3. Passover—Fiction.
4. Hametz—Fiction. 5. Jews—Fiction.] I. Hartman, Carrie, ill. II. Title.
PZ8.3.M55178lz 2012
[E]—dc23   2011014367

Manufactured in the United States of America
1 – BP – 1/1/13

IZZY the WHIZ
and PASSOVER McCLEAN

Yael Mermelstein

ILLUSTRATED BY
Carrie Hartman

KAR-BEN
PUBLISHING

Izzy the Whiz is so busy, he is

Tweaking with beakers that bubble
and fizz,

Inventing machines that can
think, blink, and talk,

Machines of your dreams that can
wiggle and walk.

Now with Passover coming, his room's filled with clutter
Like gadgets and gizmos that whistle and sputter.

Come into his world and you'll see what I mean,
   As we watch him inventing Passover McClean.

His mother came in and she said, "Izzy, please,
There's hametz all over. I'm starting to wheeze.

"The rooms are still swarming with cookies and bread,
That mouse in the corner is nibbling a shred.

There's cake in your closets and crumbs in your shoes.
Do you blame me for having pre-Passover blues?

Dear Izzy, I need to lie down in my bed,
I'm getting a bread-ache right here in my head."

"Don't worry," said Izzy "It's almost complete.
My brand new invention will make the house neat.

Go rest, take a snooze, sleep at least until two,
When I finish there won't be a thing left to chew."

A squeak and a twiddle, four drops of red ink,
A tweak and a fiddle. "It's working, I think!"

His special invention! His brand new machine!
The Super-McDuper Passover McClean!

Izzy pressed the red button, McClean lurched and whirred,
He cranked the green handle, it belched and it purred.

Then the hungry machine chomped ten books for its lunch,
Gobbled the rug, and continued to munch.

The curtains, the shelves,
   and the mattress were fed.
      To McClean, who then ate
         a large chair and a bed.

They whirled and they swirled
and they curled up inside,
Where the crumbs were all cleaned
and the toys washed and dried.

McClean then completed a quick
about face,

And spit each thing out,
put it back in its place.

Izzy checked everything with the back
of his thumb,
　　Not a flake! Not a cake!
　　Not a cookie or crumb!

Then he tugged and he lugged his machine down the stairs,
And he parked it right next to the dining room chairs.

Now Izzy would clean up the living room, too!
It would make his mom dizzy, what Izzy could do!

With a whir and a purr the machine started up,
And a fork whizzed right by with a plate and a cup.

Then a table flew by with the new cordless phone,
Then a desk, a computer, and a paperweight stone.

All were blown, all were thrown into Izzy's machine,
A pre-holiday feast for Passover McClean.

But oh my! What is this?
Smells of smoke? Reams of steam?

Then a spark! It went dark!

Oh, poor Mr. McClean!

Izzy whisked out his turbo-light, shined it about.
But it didn't look good. Things were not coming out.

He would have to tell Mother that he'd really tried,
But the living room, sadly, was stuck there inside!

But wait! Not too late! The emergency hatch!
Izzy flipped McClean over and looked for the latch.

He pulled out his super-knife-screwdriver tool,
He checked in his book for the malfunction rule.

He turned a few screws and he twisted the knife,
Then a wink and a blink and McClean came to life!

Izzy pressed the red button — Emergency Two!
And then out of the hatch
the whole living room flew!

But Izzy's wide smile sagged into a frown,
As he watched all the furniture land upside down!

The couch with its legs poking straight in the air,
An overturned table, an upside-down chair.

A carpet spread out with the rough side on top,
Light fixtures hung backwards all ready to drop.

Just then he heard slippers pad into the room!
"Oh Izzy," said Mother. He shivered with gloom.

He looked at his watch. It was just 1:15.
His mom was too early! She looked at the scene.

"Oh, goodness," she said, "but I must go back in.
I have to lie down. I can feel my head spin.

"I thought I was better," she said with a frown,
"But I'm clearly not well—the whole room's upside down!"

"What a tizzy," thought Izzy, "things couldn't be worse."
So as soon as Mom left, Izzy jammed on REVERSE.

And reverse did the trick! That McClean was so slick,
Turned the whole room right over and did it real quick.

And the house gleamed and sparkled, the room was so bright
When they sat down to seder on Passover night.

"No cookies or crumbs" said his mom, "Not a shred.
It's Passover clean—not a speck of real bread.

How beautifully dusted, how wonderfully clean."
"Thanks to him," Izzy said, as he winked at McClean.

ABOUT PASSOVER
Passover is a week-long holiday, celebrated in the spring, when we remember the exodus of the Jews from Egyptian slavery. The holiday is ushered in with a seder, a festive meal of prayers, readings, songs, and the tasting of symbolic foods.

ABOUT HAMETZ
The Torah states that all "hametz" should be removed from the home during the week of Passover. Hametz includes foods made from a mixture of flour and water that has been allowed to ferment or rise, such as bread, rolls, cookies, and pasta. Before Passover many Jewish families do a thorough cleaning to remove all hametz.

ABOUT THE AUTHOR AND ILLUSTRATOR

YAEL MERMELSTEIN is the author of *The Stupendous Adventures of Shragi and Shia* (Artscroll) and *The Car That Goes Far* (Hachai). She lives in Israel with her husband, children, pet fish, a roving flock of sheep outside her window (that does not belong to her), and her loyal pet computer. She has a band of elves (a.k.a. her children) trying to create their own McClean Machine!

CARRIE HARTMAN graduated from the Minneapolis College of Art & Design. Her illustration work includes editorial, children's books, advertising, posters, greeting cards, comic books, stationery, animation projects, and murals. Carrie lives in the Minneapolis-St. Paul area. She has 1 amazing husband, 2 pretentious pets, and 3 incredible children.